The
MYSTERIOUS MAKERS
of Shaker Street

A PICTURE'S
WORTH A THOUSAND
CLUES

The Mysterious Makers of Shaker Street
is published by Stone Arch Books,
A Capstone Imprint
1710 Roe Crest Drive
North Mankato, Minnesota 56003
www.mycapstone.com

Cataloging-in-Publication Data is available on the
Library of Congress website.

ISBN: 978-1-4965-4677-7 (library binding)
ISBN: 978-1-4965-4681-4 (paperback)
ISBN: 978-1-4965-4685-2 (eBook PDF)

Summary: The Mysterious Makers make their own version
of a drone camera and get some photos of suspicious
activity on Shaker Street.

Design Elements: Shutterstock: Master3D, PremiumVector

Designer: Tracy McCabe

Printed in Canada.
10744R

The
MYSTERIOUS MAKERS
of Shaker Street

A PICTURE'S WORTH A THOUSAND CLUES

by Stacia Deutsch
illustrated by Robin Boyden

STONE ARCH BOOKS
a capstone imprint

CHAPTER ONE

"Look at what I found!" Ten-year-old Michael Wilson popped his head out from the large, gray, metal dumpster. His brown eyes twinkled. "This is the best day ever!"

Michael's cousin, Liv Hernandez, and best friend, Leo Hammer, were waiting for him. They were in a narrow alley behind a long row of shops.

Liv leaned against the dumpster. Leo stood to the side, his hands tucked into his khaki pockets.

"I thought yesterday was the best day ever," Liv told Michael. Her dark ponytails jiggled when she laughed.

"You were super excited when we found those wooden clothespins in the dry cleaner's trash," Leo said. He was nine, a year younger than Michael and Liv.

"Yep. Yesterday was good. But today's better," Michael said. He was wearing his favorite baseball cap pulled low over his dark brown hair.

Leo had created a computer program that tracked the garbage trucks in town. They were using it to track down the fullest dumpsters.

Yesterday was the dry cleaners. Today, Michael was in the big bin behind Patsy's Arts and Crafts.

He held up two paintbrushes crusted with thick brown paint. One was very small, for fine lines. The other was big, for large blocks of color. Michael pressed his fingers against the smaller brush. The paint crumbled, like a dirt clump, into dust.

"That's some weird paint," he observed, wiping his hands on his pants.

He tossed the brushes to Leo in the alley. Leo missed them. But Liv managed to dive in for a save.

"Ah, man! I bought new paintbrushes just like these yesterday," she exclaimed, waving them around. "I can't believe you're getting them for free!"

"I'll clean them up for you," Michael said, ready to duck down and see what else he could find. "You can have these too."

Suddenly, Mr. Patterson, the owner of Patsy's Arts and Crafts, came barreling out his shop's back door. "What are you kids doing out here?" he shouted. He was wearing a business suit and holding a big black trash bag in his hands.

Mr. Patterson didn't see Michael in the dumpster. He stared at Liv and Leo. "Go away!" he boomed in a loud voice.

"We, uh, but . . . ," Leo mumbled as he backed away from Mr. Patterson.

Very quietly, behind Mr. Patterson, Michael snuck out of the dumpster.

Mr. Patterson leaned toward Leo's face. "What were you looking for? Are you spying on me?"

Leo backed up more. "I . . . I . . . we . . ." His face was flushed.

"Hey, Mr. Patterson," Michael said. He casually stepped forward. In his hands were two long narrow sticks, called dowels, and half a ball of twine. He held them out. "We're collecting trash."

"We like to make new things from old stuff," Liv boldly added, holding up the paintbrushes. "If you want, we can make you something," she offered.

Mr. Patterson was furious. He snagged the paintbrushes from Liv. "Give me those!" He anxiously looked up and down the alley. "I'm going to call the sheriff."

"I don't want to go to jail!" Leo started to run away, but Michael stopped him.

"We aren't doing anything wrong," Michael insisted. He looked at Mr. Patterson. "You threw this stuff away."

"It's still my trash. Not yours. Don't ever let me find you digging through my trash again!" Mr. Patterson told Michael. He didn't ask for the dowels or the twine back. Instead, he looked at the paintbrushes and brushed off some of the dusty paint. He stomped back to his shop and slammed the door shut.

"We should go now," Leo said with a shiver. "That was scary."

"You think everything is scary," Liv said with a laugh.

"Just one more dumpster, okay?" Michael was eyeing a red bin three doors down from the art shop. From Leo's chart, Michael knew the trash collectors hadn't come yet. That meant the bin would be full of treasures.

"Oh, come on," Leo grumbled. "What if Ms. Ventura comes out from her bridal shop to yell at us too?"

"Don't worry. She's way nicer than Mr. Patterson," Liv said, pushing up her bright red glasses. "Go on, Michael. Dive in the dumpster. We'll wait."

"I'm always outvoted." Leo sighed.

"I'll be fast," Michael said, climbing into the bridal shop's bin. He tossed a small black trash bag over the side. "Catch!"

Liv reached over Leo and snagged the bag midair.

Leo didn't even try to catch the large fabric pieces that Michael kept throwing out of the dumpster. They landed on the ground by his feet.

Liv picked up some of the fabric and took a closer look. There were long pieces of white- and cream-colored silk. She ran her hand over a large square of lace. "Are we making a wedding dress?" she asked.

"I'm not sure what we're making yet," Michael said. "We'll figure that out when we get back to the Maker Shack."

The Maker Shack was the old wooden shed in Michael's backyard. It used to be his Grandpa Henry's toolshed, but he'd given it to Michael and his friends to use as a clubhouse.

Michael climbed out of the dumpster. There was a wad of pink gum stuck to his shoe. And something that looked like moldy cheese in his hair.

"You stink," Liv said, plugging her nose.

"It's a dumpster," Michael replied with a shrug. Even if it was gross, dumpster diving was one of his favorite things to do. He shook his head, and the cheese fell to the ground. He kicked it aside then pointed at the black bag. "Did you see what I found?"

"Not yet," Liv said. She peeked inside the black trash bag. It was filled with strange rectangular items. "What are these?"

Raising a eyebrow, Michael told his friends, "Guess."

Liv held one of them up to her ear. "Is it an old kind of phone?" she asked.

"There aren't numbers to dial," Michael said, shaking his head.

"My phone doesn't have numbers on the main screen either," Liv said, putting her hands on her hips. She liked to rub it in that she had a cell phone and they didn't.

"It's a camera," Leo said. "The disposable kind. People used to hand them out at weddings, before everyone had smartphones. My parents did. They have a whole bunch of goofy photos from them." He turned the camera around in his hands. "Looks like these belong to Sarah and Paul." He showed Michael and Liv where the happy couple's name was on the side.

"The film isn't used up on these. They must have thrown out the extras," Michael said.

Liv counted the cameras. "There are twenty of them in the bag!"

"What are we going to do with twenty cameras?" Leo asked.

Each camera was a small rectangular box, plastic covered with cardboard. At the top was a small plastic viewfinder. Liv took a picture of Leo.

"Hey! I wasn't ready!" Leo complained. He ran a hand over his sandy brown hair, pushing his bangs off his eyes, and sucked in his belly. "I want to pose."

"It was a candid shot," Liv replied. She wound the film and fired off two more pictures before Leo could complain again. She took two shots of Michael. And then they gathered around the dumpster for a group selfie.

When the roll was done, Liv asked Michael, "I know there's film inside, but how do you see the pictures in one of these things?"

"We need a store to develop the film," Michael said. He wondered if there was a place that did that in the neighborhood. If not, maybe he could learn to develop film. That would be fun.

He thought that Grandpa Henry might know how. He was eighty years old and knew pretty much everything.

Michael was excited to show Grandpa the cameras. Grandpa Henry lived with Michael and his parents in their old, purple, Victorian house. The house was at the top of the hill, and Grandpa's glass windows overlooked the whole street.

"I wonder what Grandpa would do with a bag of cameras?" Michael considered as he packed them into his backpack for the trip home. It was an old blue pack he'd picked up from the trash at school.

Liv had fixed the holes in the bottom with shiny silver duct tape and written "Maker Sack" on it with extra strips of tape.

"Grandpa would probably use them to make a spaceship to the moon," Liv said, chuckling. Michael and Liv's moms were sisters, and Grandpa Henry was Michael's grandpa on his dad's side. So Liv wasn't related to Henry by blood. Still, she and Leo called him Grandpa Henry. All the kids on Shaker Street did.

"If there was a way to do that, I bet he would figure it out," Leo agreed.

"Now, we have fabric and cameras," Liv said as Michael hefted the Maker Sack onto his shoulders.

"And these dowels and a ball of twine," Michael said.

Liv was carrying the things from the art store dumpster.

"And the clothespins you found yesterday," Leo added. "Plus everything else in the Maker Shack." The shelves of the shack were filled with things that Michael and his friends had found at yard sales and in other dumpsters around town.

The trio trudged up Shaker Street. It was a big hill, and Leo liked to walk slowly.

As they walked, Michael looked up at his house. There was a large bird circling Grandpa's glass tower room. Its wings were stretched out as it soared through the sky.

Michael wondered what the bird could see from way up there.

Then suddenly he had a brilliant idea.

CHAPTER TWO

"We need scissors and ribbon," Michael told his friends.

Liv was busy emptying the Maker Sack onto the clubhouse's long workbench. The bench was made of an old door sitting on top of fruit crates. She put the camera she'd used at the dumpster to the side so it wouldn't get mixed into Michael's project.

"What are we making?" Liv asked.

"Well, I saw a bird on the way home —" Michael started.

"A bird?" Leo cut in. "Where? When?" On the way to Michael's, they'd stopped at the house where Leo and his dad rented the top floor. Leo had picked up his computer. Now, he booted it up. "Was it a bird of prey?"

"I don't think so," Michael said. He stretched out his arms. "It soared . . ."

". . . like a kite," Liv finished. She lifted the wedding dress fabric that Michael had found in the dumpster. "This'll be perfect."

"We're making a kite?" Leo asked. He leaned back in the plastic chair Michael had bought for two dollars at a garage sale. Leo's desk space was an unfinished piece of wood on two piles of bricks. "Uh, why?"

"'Cause it's fun," Liv said, rushing around the clubhouse looking for supplies. Plastic bins and cardboard boxes were stacked on shelves. She found the scissors and gave them to Michael.

"Ever heard of a bird's-eye view?" Michael asked. "I thought we'd attach one of the cameras to the kite and see what a bird sees."

Leo's fingers clicked across his keyboard. "A GPS satellite can show you exactly what's out there," he said. "Let me —"

"But don't you want to make something?" Michael asked. He pointed to a big sign on the wall.

The rules were written on cardboard in black permanent marker.

The Mysterious Makers
of Shaker Street Promise

1. We turn old things into new things.

2. We don't use new things if we can use old things.

Leo had scribbled at the bottom:
Computers are okay.

Liv had added:
Phones are okay if zombies attack. Call me!

The last line read:
This contract is legally binding.

"Couldn't we just buy a drone?" Leo asked. He was looking at shopping websites. "The mall has drones you can try. The new ones all have cameras."

"Making things is better," Michael said, pointing again at the Makers rules. "And I don't have any money, do you?"

"No, not that much," Liv said, shaking her head.

Leo patted his empty pockets and said, "I changed my mind. It's cool to make our own drone." Wanting to research something online, Leo suggested, "How about if I look for a place to develop the film?"

"Good idea," Michael said.

Liv had made a kite before. She tied the two dowels together in a cross, making sure the knots would hold tightly. Michael cut the fabric to a diamond size that fit the kite frame. Liv gathered the fabric at the ends of the dowels. She glued the fabric on to the sticks, then tied little bits of string around the fabric to hold it to the dowel.

When that was done, Liv took another piece of string and tied it loosely across the horizontal bar on the kite. She cut another piece of string and knotted it to the loose string, then attached the free end low on the long dowel.

"The kite's ready," she told Michael. "We just have to attach the ball of twine to this flying string."

Leo stood and came over to the table. He had a list in his hand. "There are a few places we can take the cameras when we're done," he said, setting down the list. "The first one is a one-hour photo-developing place."

Michael rubbed his hands together. "Our homemade drone is going to be great!" he said.

Liv added a ribbon to the bottom of the kite for balance. "Done!" she announced. She grabbed the kite and ball of twine.

"Cool," Leo said. "Let's go."

Michael didn't follow them to the door. "Hang on," he said. "We still have to attach the camera. But there's a problem."

He held one of the disposable cameras in his grip. "These cameras aren't automatic. Someone has to press the shutter to take a picture," he said.

"I can feel Michael's brain working," Liv told Leo in a whisper.

"Creepy," Leo agreed, staring at Michael.

Suddenly Michael started muttering to himself, like he did when he was hard at work on a project. "Ha," he said out loud. Then, "Aha."

Michael began running around the shack, putting things on the table.

Liv and Leo came over to investigate.

Liv picked up a strange-looking tool. "What's this?" she asked. She pressed the button and the top began to spin.

"Whoa! Be careful," Michael warned. "It's a rotary tool with a sharp cutter on top."

"What are you going to cut?" Liv asked Michael.

"One of the clothespins we found yesterday," Michael replied. He put one on the table and grabbed a pair of work goggles from a hook on the wall. He tossed the other two pairs of goggles to his friends. "This could be dangerous," he warned.

"I love danger," Liv said, putting on her goggles.

"I'll wait outside," Leo said. But he put on the goggles and stayed to see what Michael was doing. From a distance.

Michael used the rotary tool to cut off the top edge of one clothespin. With a hot glue gun he stuck the clothespin to the top of the camera.

Then he cut off the pin on the thumbtack and glued it to the clothespin, right over the shutter button.

Michael paused. The clothespin wouldn't stay open on its own. He needed to keep the clothespin and shutter button apart until they were ready to take a picture.

Leo saw the problem. He handed Michael a binder clip. "Try this," he said. "That should do the job."

The clip worked great. It kept the clothespin open.

"Now, I need two paper clips," Michael said. He held out his hand like a surgeon asking for a scalpel.

Liv handed them to him. He unbent the paper clips and glued them both to the top of the camera.

When the glue cooled, Michael ran string through the paperclips. He hung the camera from the kite.

When all that was done, Michael announced, "We're ready to fly."

CHAPTER THREE

"Whatcha doin'?" Liv's sister CoCo was standing on the sidewalk at the bottom of Shaker Street. She was wearing a bright pink leotard, a pink helmet, and had one foot on a pink scooter.

"We're going to fly a kite," Liv told her sister as the boys got the kite ready. Leo unwound the ball of twine. Michael held the kite.

Michael, Leo, and Liv had chosen Liv's house because it was the flattest part of the street. Liv had lived there with her mom and sister ever since her parents' divorce. Her dad lived a block over.

"Why?" CoCo asked. She was five years old and super chatty.

"Kites are fun," Liv said for the second time that day. But then she had a question of her own. "Aren't you supposed to be at gymnastics with Dad?"

"I already went," CoCo replied, rolling her eyes at Liv, as if she should have known. "He just dropped me off. Mom's inside. She's busy painting."

Liv's mom loved to paint. It was her hobby, and she was pretty good. At least that's what Michael's mom said. Michael didn't understand art that looked like paint splatters.

"Art is in the our blood," Liv said, looking toward the house. Michael knew that wasn't true. His aunt — Liv's mom — had been painting for a year. His mom never painted, as far as he knew. And Liv had just started her first art class at the local museum the week before.

"In class this week, Mrs. Patterson told me to follow my dreams," Liv said.

Mrs. Patterson was Liv's art teacher. She was also the mother of Mr. Patterson — the grumpy owner of the arts and crafts store. And she was Liv's neighbor. But, unlike her son, Mrs. Patterson was nice. Liv told them, "I've been dreaming about a ninja warrior in black clothes. I'm going to paint her sneaking through a dark room."

"Uh, that's an all black painting, right?" Leo asked.

"You just don't understand art," Liv told Leo. "It might look like black paint to you. But real artists will know it's a ninja at night."

"Oh, check out that wind!" Michael changed the subject. He didn't want them to start arguing. He licked his finger and raised it. "The wind is coming from the north. We better get started."

Liv held the kite.

CoCo sat on the grass to watch.

Michael held the string that went to the camera and attached to the binder clip.

Leo checked that the clothespin was still above the shutter.

There was only one job left to do. Everyone looked at Leo.

"Bah." Leo knew that meant he'd been chosen to run and actually fly the kite.

He took the ball of string and muttered,
"I always get the worst jobs." Taking a deep
breath, he started running with the string.

"Wahoo!" CoCo shouted as Liv released the kite when it was time. It soared into the air.

They let it get above the trees in Liv's yard and hover there for a little while.

Michael was so happy. It really was a great day for flying a kite. When the kite was high enough, he tugged on his string. The binder clip snapped off. There was a faint click when the clothespin pressed the thumbtack, which hit the shutter.

"If that worked like I planned, we have our first photo!" Michael cheered.

"Do it again!" CoCo told Michael. "Take more pictures! Take one of my room!"

"Okay!" Michael looked up at the kite and then stared down at the blinder clip attached to the string in his hand. "Oh . . . wait. Hmm."

"Hmm?" Liv stopped dancing. "What is it?"

Michael clicked his tongue. "There's a problem." He explained, "The film winds manually. We have to bring down the kite and wind the camera."

"We have to start over?" Leo sighed heavily. "I have to run with the kite again?"

"Do it again, Leo!" CoCo spun around. "More pictures! More!"

"It's a good thing," Michael told Leo. "There are fifteen shots on the camera. This way, we can move up the street and get a lot of different viewpoints."

"Fifteen photos? That means I have to run fifteen times to get the kite up!" Leo gasped for air. "I think I hear my dad calling," he said, raising a hand to his ear. "I gotta go."

"What are you complaining about?' Liv asked him. "It's not that hard."

"Not hard for you to hold the kite!" Leo said, "But I have to run fifteen times! And on the hill too. Go ahead, call an ambulance." He put his hand against his chest and swayed. "I'll need it."

"Oh, Leo, you should be an actor! We can take turns," Liv told him.

"I want to help too!" CoCo said.

Michael mapped the photos they were going to take. "Fifteen shots means we can take seven on each side of the street, and one over my house at the top."

"We can move higher up the hill each time, and always run down," Liv suggested.

That made Leo feel better. He held out the ball of string. "Who's running next?"

Michael took the next turn and then Liv. Finally it was CoCo's turn.

Michael tied the kite string to her scooter handlebars. CoCo rode her scooter instead of running with the string. Leo let go of the kite when the string was tight and it soared high. Michael took the picture.

When her kite came back down, CoCo wasn't out of breath like the rest of them. After that, they all used the scooter.

It wasn't long before they were standing at the top, in Michael's front yard, taking the last shot of the day.

"I'll get my computer," Leo said. It was in the Maker Shack. "Let's get this to the film shop. They can give us the pictures digitally when they're ready. We can download them right away."

Leo packed the computer into his backpack. Liv put away the kite. Michael put the used camera in the Maker Sack and hung it over his shoulders.

"I know how to get there!" CoCo said, proudly. They gave her the important job of leading the way.

They were all tired and a little sweaty when they headed to the photo shop.

As they neared the bottom of the hill, Mr. Patterson came out of his mother's house, onto the sidewalk. They weren't surprised to see him as he visited her often.

What was surprising was that he was so messy. He'd changed clothes. Now, he was wearing jeans and a T-shirt that was splattered with light blue and brown paint. There was red paint on his shoes and yellow speckles in his hair.

"Did you fly a kite above my mother's house?" he asked, standing in a way that blocked the sidewalk. He pointed back at the green house behind him.

"Yes," Liv said confidently while Leo moved behind her. Michael saw him tighten his backpack straps. Leo always did that when he was getting ready to run.

"I noticed you moving up the street as you flew it," he said, narrowing his eyes. "What exactly were you doing?"

Leo whispered to the others, "He seems mad. Do you think he'll call Sheriff Kawasaki?"

"Calm down. It'll be okay," Michael assured Leo.

"We took pictures!" CoCo told Mr. Patterson happily.

She flapped her arms like wings. "We are going to see what a bird sees," she added.

"I want those pictures," Mr. Patterson said, holding his hand out toward them. "Give them to me."

Leo was scared, but he also knew some stuff about the law from his dad, who was a lawyer.

"GPS sites take photos from the sky all the time," he told Michael softly. "There's no law that stops a satellite, and," Leo whispered, "it could be argued in court that our kite is like a satellite or drone."

"What are you kids yapping about?" Mr. Patterson demanded, "Tell me!"

Michael loudly repeated everything Leo had whispered.

"Really?" Mr. Patterson lowered his eyes.

He looked like he was going to grab Michael's backpack and snatch it away.

"We don't have them, anyway," Michael said, which was technically true. They had a camera and film, but no pictures. Not yet anyway.

Suddenly Mrs. Patterson called out the door to the house. "There's a phone call for you! They want to make a deal."

Mr. Patterson looked at his mother, then back at the kids. He was clearly in a hurry to take the call. He said, "When you get them, bring them here." With a huff, Mr. Patterson went back inside, leaving the kids on the street.

"Bye!" CoCo waved to Mr. Patterson's back.

"We aren't giving him the photos, are we?" Leo asked Michael and Liv.

"No," Michael said. "Maybe if he'd asked nicely, we'd show them to him. But that was seriously weird."

Liv looked at the Patterson house. She muttered, "Strange times on Shaker Street." Then louder, "We gotta get that film developed." Liv bent down in a runner's pose and told CoCo, "Let's race. I'll beat you there!"

Michael and Leo didn't run with them. Instead they walked slowly behind the girls.

"What do you think that was all about?" Leo asked Michael.

Michael shrugged. "It's like Liv said, there's something strange going on." He put a hand on his Maker Sack. "It looks like we've stumbled on a mystery."

CHAPTER FOUR

Michael watched Liv pace around the photo shop. It was going to be an hour before their pictures were ready.

"What's going on?" Liv muttered in a husky voice. She wasn't really talking to Michael or Leo, so they just let her talk to herself. She mumbled questions like, "Why doesn't Mr. Patterson want us to have photos of his yard? Why was he so weird about the dumpster?"

CoCo answered every question with, "I don't know."

Liv checked her watch every few minutes. "The hour to get the photos feels like forever," she complained.

"Let's kill time at the art museum," Michael suggested.

"Great idea," Liv said, opening the film shop door.

The neighborhood museum was a few blocks down. Again, CoCo led the way.

When they entered the large, historic manor, Leo complained, "This place is boring. And I don't get why you have to whisper."

"It's respectful to the other people," Liv told him.

"What other people?" Leo asked, looking around the room. They were the only ones in the museum.

Michael checked out some small portraits and a big picture of a lady with an umbrella. "I remember coming here last year in school," he said.

"It was the most boring field trip ever," Leo said.

"You are both so uncultured," Liv told them, pushing up her glasses for a better look at a pencil sketch. "I think this might be a picture of the night that aliens invaded town."

"That never happened," Michael told Liv. He came to take a closer look. "I think it's a picture of spaghetti. Hard to tell." He walked away.

Since Liv liked the museum, she knew a few things. "Let's go see the oldest and most valuable piece of art they have," she said.

The boys and CoCo followed her into a small side room.

There, alone in the middle of a big wall, was a painting of two women sewing. The window in the picture was open, filling the room with yellow sunlight. One woman had red fabric in her hands. There was a child on the brown wooden floor in a faded blue dress.

"I love this painting," Liv gushed. "It's like four hundred years old."

"Four hundred years! Wow! It must be worth a lot of money," Michael said.

"Millions!" Liv agreed. "Maybe billions."

Leo, Liv, and CoCo went on to the next room, but Michael stopped.

A powder on the floor caught his eye. He
bent down and touched it. The dark brown
dust felt like there were bits of sand in it.
Michael noticed that the trail of dust led
back to the rare painting. There was a lot of
the brown dirt under the picture. When he
looked close at the art again, he saw that the
corner of the painting was crumbling.

"That's strange," he said to himself. "I guess our small town doesn't have enough money for repair. I bet it would cost a lot to fix this up."

Michael rushed to catch up with Liv, Leo, and CoCo, who were ready to go get the photos. "They must be done by now," Liv said, heading to the exit.

Liv went in the shop alone, while the others waited by the door. "You aren't going to believe this!" she said, coming out. She waved the package of photos in the air.

"What?" Leo asked. He tried to take the packet of photos from Liv, but she pulled them away.

"First, I have printed pictures and a code for downloads," she said, sitting down on a park bench.

Leo put out his hand, silently asking for the code. She didn't give it right away. Instead, Liv took out the printed photos.

"Here's Michael's house." She gave Michael a blurry shot of his backyard. Someone was standing by the Maker Shack. Even though the shot was blurry, the kids knew it had to be Grandpa Henry.

Michael sighed, saying, "I wonder what he's up to." Grandpa liked to pull pranks on Michael and his friends.

Michael squinted at the shot. It was impossible to tell if the old man was bending down, messing with the locks on the shack, or standing on his tiptoes, closer to the tree. Maybe both. It might be a few days, but soon enough, Michael was certain, they'd find out what he was doing.

The next shot Liv showed them was too blurry to make out. "The wind wiggled the kite too much on that one," Leo said, peeking over at the picture.

They scanned through a couple more pictures of trees and rooftops.

"Where's the mystery?" Leo asked.

"Where's the mystery?" CoCo repeated. "Mysteries are fun!"

"They are fun," Liv said as she ruffled her sister's hair. "That's why I saved the most interesting one for last."

She handed Michael the photo they'd taken in front of the Pattersons' house.

"It's a good picture," Leo said. He was proud of the way he'd held the kite steady while Michael pulled the binder clip off the camera. "Nice and clear."

The picture was a bird's view looking down over the Patterson roof and backyard. The house next door was also in the frame.

After studying the picture for a few minutes, Leo asked Liv, "Is Mrs. Patterson moving?"

"No!" Liv said. "That's what makes it so strange."

Michael took the photo and studied it. "If Mrs. Patterson isn't moving, what are all these boxes and that tall crate doing in her backyard?"

"I don't know!" Liv lowered her voice to a spooky whisper. "That's the mystery!"

Leo put his computer on his lap. "Let an expert take a look," he said, booting up the laptop. He held out his hand and said, "In case you didn't know, I'm the expert."

Liv and Michael laughed. Liv gave Leo the photo shop website address and code.

Michael was anxious to see if they could zoom in on Mrs. Patterson's backyard.

"One more second . . . ," Leo announced. "Got it." He pointed at the image on the screen. "She's got one large rectangular crate in the yard. And a lot of boxes." There were enough boxes to pack up a whole house.

"Are you sure she's not moving?" Michael asked Liv. "She's old enough to retire."

"No way. That old lady isn't going anywhere." Liv shook her head. "My mom told me that Mrs. Patterson is going to work at the museum forever."

"How does she know?" Leo asked.

"Mrs. Patterson told her when we signed up for the art classes," Liv replied.

Then she added, "Mrs. Patterson said she needed to make more money. She couldn't afford to quit working."

"Interesting," Michael said. He looked again at the picture. The boxes looked like regular moving boxes, but that crate was unusual. It was narrow and tall — about four feet high and two feet long. What would fit in that?

And more importantly, was this the photo Mr. Patterson didn't want them to have? Mr. Patterson wasn't even in the picture. There weren't any people in the photo. Just boxes.

"We need to investigate," Liv said. "Let's go back to Mrs. Patterson's house."

"That doesn't seem like a good idea," Leo protested. "We can't snoop around the backyard. That's illegal. The sheriff might really arrest us then."

"We can knock on the door," Liv said. "I have a painting I made last week after class. We could take it to show Mrs. Patterson. Maybe she'll invite us in."

"Then we can look around," Michael announced, liking the idea.

Liv said, "Let's drop CoCo off at my house and get my painting," Liv whispered, so CoCo wouldn't hear that she was going to be left behind. Then she added, "Remember, Sheriff Kawasaki would want us to find out what's going on."

A few weeks earlier, they'd discovered a thief digging tunnels under Shaker Street toward the bank and the vault. They'd stopped the thief, and since then, Liv was convinced that it was up to them to help the sheriff stop crime. Leo and Michael weren't so sure, but Liv was sure enough for all three of them.

When they got to Liv's house, Liv's mom asked her to watch CoCo for a few more hours.

"We're stuck with her," Liv said when they both came back outside.

"I'm going to be a detective!" CoCo announced, skipping along with them to Mrs. Patterson's.

"First rule of being a detective," Michael said, "is not telling anyone what you're doing."

CoCo zipped her lips and threw away the key. Then she said, "We're secret detectives."

"Good," Michael said with a laugh.

When they reached Mrs. Patterson's house, Leo had a thought. "What if Mr. Patterson answers the door? He's going to want our photos."

"I don't have them anymore," Liv responded, feeling clever. "I left them at home when I got the painting."

Leo gripped his laptop against his chest. "Well, I'm not giving him my computer," he said.

"Maybe we should stay away from him," Michael said. "Is there a way to find out if Mr. Patterson is still there?"

"I don't see his van," Liv said. Mr. Patterson's van was big and white and had "Patsy's Arts and Crafts" painted on it. "But it could be in the garage," Liv pointed out.

They decided to move to the other side of the street, just in case Mr. Patterson saw them standing there.

"I'll go peek inside the window," Liv offered.

When she was at home, she'd taken the time to wrap her painting in brown paper and tape the edges like a present. The package was taller than CoCo and about as wide as Michael and Leo standing together. "I'll let you know if I see him," Liv told the others.

"CoCo," she told her sister, "stay here with Michael and Leo."

Before Leo could tell Liv it was a very dangerous, super bad idea, Liv handed Michael her painting and dashed across the street.

She was back in a flash. "Want to hear something weird?" she asked.

"Probably not," Leo replied. "Is it weird funny or weird scary? Answer that and then I'll decide."

"The glass isn't clear." Liv went on as if Leo never spoke. "I walk by this house every day. I can't believe I never noticed before, but you can't see through the windows to the inside."

"Oh. That *is* weird," Michael said. He handed Liv back her painting.

"How will we find out if Mr. Patterson is there or not?" Liv sighed.

"There's a way," Leo said, staring at Liv's painting. "I know how to see through frosted windows!"

CHAPTER FIVE

Leo peeled off a small strip of tape from Liv's painting package.

"Hey!" she exclaimed. "What are you doing?"

Leo said, "This tape will make a frosted window look clear." He handed her a small piece.

"How's that gonna work?" Liv asked.

Michael knew.

"Frosted glass has a lot of little scratches on it, making it hard to see through," he explained. "The tape fills the scratches, making it clear."

"Cool," Liv said, holding the tape to the sunlight. "Be right back!"

She dashed across the street again.

"I'm so nervous," Leo muttered, staring at the front porch of the house. They could see Liv searching for a good spot to look through.

She found a place on the side of the front door. She put the tape on the glass and peeked through the tiny spot.

When she didn't come back right away, Michael said to Leo, "She's been there too long. I think something's wrong."

When Liv turned back to them, she had a look of horror on her face. She signaled the two of them to come — quick.

Michael carried her painting across the street and up the Pattersons' narrow porch steps. Leo and his heavy backpack got there a second later.

"Look," Liv gasped.

"Is Mr. Patterson inside?" Leo stepped back down the first step. "He'll have us arrested for trespassing, then arrested again for taking pictures of his yard." He sighed. "There are probably some other arresting things that I'm not thinking of."

"No one's getting arrested," Michael assured him. "We're just standing here." He looked inside through Liv's tape. "Oh no!" he cried.

"I know!" Liv said, moving aside so Leo could take a look as well.

Leo glanced up and down the street, in case Sheriff Kawasaki was on her way. When he saw that no one was coming, he peered through the small piece of tape into Mrs. Patterson's window.

"Is that CoCo?" Leo asked Liv.

Liv nodded. "She was supposed to stay with you and Michael, but she didn't."

None of them noticed when she'd gone across the street.

Now CoCo was inside Mrs. Patterson's house. It looked like they were having tea and cookies!

"I'm the worst babysitter ever," Liv moaned. "I lost my sister."

"She's not lost," Michael said. "We know where she is."

"We gotta save her," Liv said, her voice panicked. "What if Mr. Patterson is holding her ransom? What it he wants us to trade the pictures for the kid? What will I do?"

"Tell him you don't have the pictures," Michael said. And it was true.

"I'll hide the computer," Leo added. He ran a few houses up the street and put his backpack in his own front yard under a bush. "It's safe. We can tell the truth. We don't have any pictures anymore."

"Okay. Let's get CoCo," Liv said. She pressed the door buzzer.

"Hello, Liv," Mrs. Patterson greeted them as she opened the door. "Michael. Leo. It's nice to see you all."

She stepped aside to let them in. "I rarely get visitors," she added.

CoCo was sitting at a small table covered with a lace cloth. "We're having a snack!" she said happily.

"What are you doing here?" Liv leaned into her sister and whispered, "You were supposed to stay by the tree."

"I'm a detective!" CoCo said. "Detectives don't wait around."

"Yes they do," Liv told her and then nudged her sister to be quiet.

Michael looked around for any sign that Mr. Patterson was in the house. If he was, why hadn't he come to find them? Earlier he had seemed desperate to get their film.

Mrs. Patterson didn't ask about any pictures or cameras.

Michael watched her get more sugar for CoCo's tea. Mrs. Patterson's hair was white and her skin wrinkled. He wondered how old she actually was.

The furniture in the house looked like it had been there forever. The couch was dusty, and there was an old typewriter in the corner. He really wanted to go check out the typewriter. Michael had to look away to stop his own curiosity.

"So what exactly are you kids investigating?" Mrs. Patterson asked CoCo, setting down the sugar bowl. She looked up at the others and said with a smile, "We haven't discussed the mystery yet."

"We're gonna have tea first," CoCo said. "I never had tea before."

"Would you also like some?" Mrs. Patterson asked Liv, Leo, and Michael.

"No, thank you," Michael replied.

"I bet it's poisoned," Leo whispered to Liv, moving back from the table.

"I'll check. If I drop dead, you'll know why," Liv whispered back. Before Leo could knock the cup away, Liv quickly leaned over and took a sip of CoCo's tea. "Oh. Yum," she said.

"Not poisoned," she told Leo. Then she handed the cup back to her sister. "You'll like it, CoCo." She refused a cup of her own, saying, "Thank you. It's delicious, but I'm not thirsty."

Mrs. Patterson looked to CoCo and said, "Now, you were going to tell me about the mystery."

"We took bird pictures," CoCo said. "And we saw —"

"Oof!" To stop CoCo from talking, Liv knocked into the table. The tea spilled onto the cloth. "Oh, I'm so sorry," Liv apologized to Mrs. Patterson, grabbing CoCo's napkin to mop up the light yellow spill.

"It's all right, dear," Mrs. Patterson said calmly, getting some paper towels.

"If you put salt on the spill right away, it won't stain the cloth," Michael suggested.

Mrs. Patterson nodded. "Clever boy!"

"He makes stuff," CoCo started.

"For the mystery?" Mrs. Patterson asked, trying again to get CoCo to share.

"We —" CoCo started.

Before CoCo could reveal that they'd seen strange boxes in the backyard, Liv grabbed her painting. Michael had set it against the wall when they'd first come into the kitchen.

"Mrs. Patterson!" Liv interrupted. "I have been dying to show you what I made after our art class last week."

Liv ripped off the paper to show a large, brown painted square.

Mrs. Patterson stared at the painting for a long moment. "That's very interesting," she said at last.

"It's a brown canvas," Leo said, a little surprised to finally be seeing Liv's masterpiece. "Is that all?"

"You really don't understand art," Liv proclaimed. She waved him away. "It's not a brown canvas. It's a picture of Bigfoot swimming in a mud puddle."

"Ah," Mrs. Patterson said, leaning in for a closer look. "I see that now."

"I'm going to do a series that goes together," Liv told her. "Next is 'Ninja in the Dark.' After that, I'll make a 'Mummy in Snow.'" Liv smiled. "Maybe we can hang them up at the museum when I'm done?"

Mrs. Patterson was quiet for a long moment. Then said, "I'm sorry, dear. Today was my last day. I don't work at the museum anymore."

CHAPTER SIX

For a moment, Michael wondered if it was an excuse. Mrs. Patterson probably didn't want to hang Liv's strange pictures. But the look on her face showed that she was serious.

"I've never had enough money to travel. I've always wanted to though," she told them. "I want to live in France. Go to museums. Study great painters."

"Are you going soon?" Michael asked.

"Yes," she said. "Tomorrow morning, I'm getting paid for a project. My son and I have been working on it for a long time. Right after I get paid, I'm going to move to France."

She glanced over her shoulder toward the basement door. Michael noticed. But he wasn't sure what she was looking at.

Liv protested, "You can't go away. We just started the class."

Michael remembered Liv saying that Mrs. Patterson had told them she wasn't going to retire or move. Clearly everything had changed in the past few days.

"Someone else will take over." Mrs. Patterson refilled CoCo's teacup, even though it was mostly full.

"Will Mr. Patterson teach the class?" Michael asked.

It made sense because he owned the arts and crafts store. His own paintings hung in the windows.

"Oh, gosh, no. My son's coming with me. I'm selling the house." She looked at Michael. "I was going to call your mother about it next week. Just settling some details and —"

Suddenly there was a thud from downstairs.

"Uh, is Mr. Patterson here?" Leo asked. His voice squeaked.

Mrs. Patterson looked confused at his question. She must not have heard the sound. But when it happened again, she stood and stomped her foot.

Michael wondered if she was sending a warning to someone in the basement.

"Well, children, time for you to go," Mrs. Patterson said, rising. She took away CoCo's full teacup. Walking fast, she ushered them toward the door. Michael noticed that she didn't ask about their investigations again.

As they passed a long hallway, Michael heard the sound one more time. It was like a can knocking over. And he swore he heard a man grunt.

He shook his head. If Mr. Patterson wasn't there, someone else was.

They reached the front door. "Well, goodbye," Mrs. Patterson said. She looked out to the street then said quietly, "You know how detectives keep secrets?"

CoCo nodded.

"Can you keep it a secret that I am leaving town, please?" Mrs. Patterson asked. "I haven't told anyone at the museum yet."

But she didn't wait for an answer. Pushing them gently outside, Mrs. Patterson shut the door quickly.

When they were standing on the porch, Liv held her Bigfoot painting close to her chest. "She's the best art teacher I've ever had," she said sadly.

"She's the only art teacher you've had," Leo said, then stopped when he noticed something strange. He pointed to CoCo's shoe and asked her, "What's that?"

CoCo sat down on the sidewalk and took off her left shoe. She looked closely at the spot, then said, "It's brown paint!"

Leo looked closely at the paint color. He touched it, then looked at his finger. "Hmm," he said.

"Hmm, what?" Liv asked.

"I think I've seen this paint color before,"
Leo said. "Let's go get my computer. I want
to check it out."

CHAPTER SEVEN

At the Maker Shack, Michael asked CoCo for her shoe. He turned it over in his hands. The paint was dry, but crumbled a little when he picked at it with his nail.

"Is this the kind of paint you use in class?" he asked Liv, handing her the shoe.

"No," Liv answered right away. "This is thicker. It has a weird powder in it."

Leo was already at his computer station, booted up. "Would you call that light or dark brown?"

"Dark," Liv said, while CoCo plopped down into Liv's beanbag chair. She went over to look at Leo's computer screen. "Is that the museum's website?" she asked.

"Yes," Leo said. "I was thinking about the colors in the painting we saw today. There was a girl playing on a brown floor, while two women sewed. One was wearing a pale blue dress. And there was red fabric."

Liv said, "I thought you said the museum was boring."

Leo shrugged. "I decided that sewing picture that wasn't so bad. It was cool that it was four hundred years old. I'm going to look it up. The brown on CoCo's shoe looks familiar."

81

He read for a few minutes, then said, "Whoa! Did you know that painting was painted with a color called mummy brown?"

"Mummy brown!" Liv exclaimed. "That sounds fantastic!"

"It sounds cool, but it doesn't have anything to do with real mummies," Michael said. He was only half listening to them. He was busy sorting through all his disposable cameras.

"No, Michael. The paint was made with actual mummy!" Leo replied, then said, "Ewww." He read more about the picture. "About four hundred years ago, they used to mix bits of ground-up mummy cats and humans into it." Leo shuddered.

"I can't believe I didn't know this!" Liv said. "I like that painting even more now!"

Leo said, "There aren't a lot of spare mummies lying around, so they don't make that kind of paint anymore. But I was thinking, what if someone could make a really good copy of that painting?"

Michael said, "You could steal the original then sell it for a million dollars."

"Or more," Liv added.

Michael nodded and said, "But everyone would know if you tried to fake that brown color paint. Mummy brown needs mummy ashes in it. Where would you get a mummy?"

"You probably don't need it," Leo said. With fast fingers, he typed in a website and read what he found. "Today artists use a mixture of goethite and hematite with quartz and kaolin to create the same look. These are minerals made of iron and clay."

He read to himself, then looked up. "It says they can be crushed together to make the exact right color and consistency."

"That's too bad," Liv said, frowning. "Real mummy parts would be cool. You could make finger paints with ancient fingers!"

Leo laughed.

Suddenly, Michael's eyes went wide. "All the clues add up! That kind of crumbly paint was on the brushes in Mr. Patterson's art store trash dump. It was also on the museum floor! There's a mysterious tall crate in Mrs. Patterson's yard, just the right size for a painting. Fake mummy brown paint was on CoCo's shoe after she left the Patterson house!"

Michael looked at his friends and declared, "Mrs. Patterson and her son are art thieves!"

CHAPTER EIGHT

"The Pattersons are going to make a copy of the famous painting — then steal the original!" Liv said, figuring it out with Michael.

"This doesn't sound right," Leo noted. "Mrs. Patterson liked working at the museum."

"She wants to move to France," Michael reminded his friend.

"France is expensive," CoCo put in. "I told Mom I wanted to see the Awful Tower and she said it was too much money to get there."

"It's the Eiffel Tower," Liv corrected her.

"That's true." Michael added, "But if the Pattersons sell the museum's mummy art, they'll have plenty of money. Mrs. Patterson said they were getting paid tomorrow for a project. I think that means they already know someone who wants to buy the original piece!"

"I bet that was the phone call he got after we took pictures," Liv put in. "Mrs. Patterson said something about a 'deal' and then Mr. Patterson rushed inside."

"We have to call Sheriff Kawasaki," Leo said. "Right now."

"We need proof first," Liv told him. "We have a lot of clues, but we don't have any facts."

Michael held up the disposable cameras. "Mrs. Patterson said they are leaving town tomorrow. My guess is that they are switching the paintings tonight after the museum closes!"

"What are we going to do?" Liv asked. She asked CoCo to stop singing some French song she'd heard on TV. "Shhh," Liv told CoCo.

CoCo kept singing, only softer.

"We need to swap the fake art with another painting before they get to the museum," Michael said.

"How are we going to do that?" Leo asked.

"And what are we going to do with the fake art?" Liv asked. "Whatever we swap it with has to be the same size so they don't notice until it's too late."

Michael considered both questions. "Leo's question first," he said. He held up the bag of disposable cameras. "We'll make a distraction with these." He held up a roll of strong silver tape. "And this."

"Okay, but what sort of distraction?" Leo pressed.

"A strobe light," Michael said. "You know — the kind of light that keeps on flashing."

Michael wrote down a list of the rest of the things he needed to make strobe lights. Liv and Leo ran around the shack collecting everything.

This was a big project, and they didn't have a lot of time. Michael needed a soldering iron, electrical tape, small batteries, electronic switches, and wire.

"I'm amazed at everything that Michael knows how to do," Liv said as they watched him at work. He took apart the cameras, removed the flash circuit, and created trigger wires.

"I want to make it so all we have to do is push a button and the camera's flashbulb won't stop blinking until we turn it off," said Michael.

"Cool, but why do we need flashing lights?" Liv asked.

"Yeah, why?" CoCo echoed.

Michael smiled and said, "You'll see."

When it started to get dark, Leo and Liv walked CoCo home. She wanted to stay to see the strobe lights, but it was getting late. Michael stayed back to work on the project.

When they got back, Liv and Leo went in to have dinner with Michael's parents and Grandpa Henry.

Michael skipped dinner and kept working. They brought him a piece of pizza. He ate and worked.

It took a few more hours until he was done. By then it was dark outside.

"I'm ready," Michael told his friends, putting all of the remade cameras into his Maker Sack. "Bring your Bigfoot picture, Liv. We'll need it!"

They hurried down the hill to Mrs. Patterson's house. When they arrived, the Patsy's Arts and Crafts truck was pulling into the driveway.

"We're too late," Liv whispered from their spot behind a bush.

"No, we aren't," Michael assured her. "He just arrived. That means they haven't put the fake art into the crate yet."

"Are we going to stop them with the strobe lights?" Liv asked.

Michael tapped the Maker Sack. "Yes. I have a plan." They snuck around to the backyard. "We have to wait until they load the truck." He nodded toward Liv, who was holding her painting. "We're going to make a distraction. And you're going to trade the Pattersons' art for the Bigfoot painting, okay?"

"What happens when the Pattersons discover the switch?" Liv asked, looking fondly at her painting. "Will I ever see my painting again?" she wondered.

"I don't know," Michael said truthfully.

"I hate to give up Bigfoot," she said. "It's my first masterpiece."

"Hopefully nothing happens to it, but remember you'll be helping the museum. Saving something with real mummy in it," Michael said, knowing that would probably convince her.

"Goodbye, Bigfoot," Liv said, getting over her sadness. She raised her head. "When this is over, I'm going to try to talk to the mummy-ghost in the mummy-art," she declared. "I'm sure that painting is haunted."

"I'll skip the séance," Leo said.

"I need you to run the computer," Liv told him. "Talking to ghosts is all technical these days."

Leo sighed. "As long as Michael comes too," he said.

"Ghosts don't exist. Not even mummy ghosts," Michael said firmly as he emptied his backpack.

He'd made eight blinking strobe lights. He handed four to Leo.

"Let's focus on stopping the thieves," Michael said. They went around the back of the Pattersons' house and used the silver duct tape to attach separate camera strobes to the trees.

"When I give the signal, start pressing the buttons on the cameras," Michael told Leo.

Michael continued, "They don't take pictures anymore. I made it so the flashbulbs just blink."

The kids waited quietly until the van was loaded with the narrow crate. Liv, Leo, and Michael were certain that the fake mummy brown painting was inside.

If it was a good enough copy, no one at the museum would ever know the real one had been switched.

Mr. Patterson closed the van door then went around to get in the driver's seat.

"Sasquatch!" Michael whispered the signal.

Leo pressed the button on the disposable camera closest to him. The flashbulb began to blink off and on.

"What's that?" Mr. Patterson asked aloud, looking over toward the trees by the side of the backyard. He took a step in that direction, when suddenly from the other side of the yard, Michael started flashing lights with a different camera.

Michael and Leo went back and forth like that until the entire area behind the Patterson house was filled with flashing bulbs, like a disco.

"What's going on?" Mrs. Patterson asked, coming out the back door. She was wearing black pants, a black shirt, and a black hat. Mr. Patterson was dressed the same way.

"I don't know, Mother," Mr. Patterson replied.

The two of them stared at all of the flashing lights.

That was when Liv snuck into action.

While the Pattersons were shielding their eyes from the blinding lights and trying to figure out what was going on, Liv opened the back of the van. She traded the fake artwork with her own Bigfoot art. Then she closed the van door.

A few minutes later, the camera flashes suddenly stopped when Michael and Leo turned them off.

Mr. Patterson and his mom stared out in the darkness, but didn't search the yard.

Mrs. Patterson said, "It looks like those Smith boys are having a wild party again. The flashing lights are probably part of the decorations. Next, I bet loud music is about to start." She groaned.

"I'll deal with those boys when we get back," said Mr. Patterson. "Right now, Mom, we have to hurry." Michael heard him mutter something about being happy to be moving away.

Mr. Patterson slammed the doors to the van. His mom got into her seat. Moments later, they drove off toward the museum.

Michael and Leo collected the cameras.

Liv took the Pattersons' fake mummy art home and put it in her garage.

Leo and Michael were ready to run to the museum, but Liv stopped them.

"We have to do one more thing first," Liv said as they got to the bottom of the street. "We need to get the sheriff."

CHAPTER NINE

"Stay here," the sheriff told Liv, Leo, and Michael. She pointed to a spot near the Patsy's Arts and Crafts van.

She had two other officers meet her at the museum. They were about to rush into the museum. "Tell me again where this rare painting is?" the sheriff asked Liv. "We don't want to turn on the lights. We need to surprise the thieves," she explained.

"It's a left, then a right, then back two steps and another right and then . . . ," Liv began.

"Would it be easier if we showed you?" Michael asked the sheriff.

"Fine," the sheriff gave in. "But you need to stay behind me."

"I don't think this is a good —" Leo began, but Liv grabbed his arm.

"Let's go," Liv said. Then to the sheriff she whispered, "Turn left inside the door."

They all snuck toward the mummy brown painting.

Suddenly there was a scuffling noise heading their way. It sounded like shoes against a tile floor.

The sheriff shouted to the kids, "Duck! Out of the way!" Leo was the first one down. Liv and Michael dropped on top of him in a pile.

The sheriff flipped on a big flashlight. She pointed the beam at two people, dressed in black. They were carrying a tall, narrow crate.

"Hello, Mrs. Patterson. And Mr. Patterson," the sheriff said. "Mind telling us what's in the box?" she asked. Her officers turned on the museum lights.

"This?" Mrs. Patterson asked, setting down her side of the crate. "Well, it's . . . ," she stalled.

Mr. Patterson set down his side too. They leaned the crate against the wall. "You see, we heard there was an art thief coming to rob the museum. So we're taking the original painting to our house for safety," he explained.

The sheriff looked at him suspiciously.

"We left an exact copy," Mr. Patterson said. "So the thieves would be confused."

"So you're protecting the art?" Sheriff Kawasaki asked.

"Exactly," both Pattersons said at the same time.

The sheriff turned to Michael. "I have to let them go. We will investigate more tomorrow, but I can't hold them tonight without proof. Their answer explains why they are moving the famous art."

"But it's not true," Michael said, stepping forward. "We already switched the paintings, so that they couldn't steal the original!"

"Hmm . . . I need to see the copy of the artwork," the sheriff said, curious.

Liv led them all to the room where the rare painting had been hanging.

There, in the middle of a large wall was Liv's Bigfoot painting. It had been dark in the museum. The Pattersons hadn't noticed that what they were putting up on the wall was different than the painting they were stealing.

"My art is on display!" Liv said, more excited about that than having caught two art thieves.

"Where's my painting?" Mr. Patterson asked, turning to Liv with an angry look. "I've been working on the perfect brown color for a year!"

"Too bad you didn't have any mummies," Liv replied.

"We have pictures to prove that they were trying to steal the famous painting," Michael told the sheriff. "They have moving boxes in their backyard."

"They told us they are getting paid for a project," Liv said. "Lots of money."

Leo added, "And Mrs. Patterson said that they are going to France in the morning."

"All the clues add up," Michael said. "The Pattersons aren't going to protect the painting. They are going to sell it and move to France."

"But now you've spoiled everything!" Mrs. Patterson yelled at Liv, Michael, and Leo.

With that, the old woman confirmed everything they suspected. The officers put handcuffs on her and her son.

Michael, Liv, and Leo waited outside while the thieves were arrested. When it was over, Sheriff Kawasaki came over to them.

"I talked to the museum director," she said. "He's been traveling a lot lately. So he gave more responsibility to Mrs. Patterson. But she took advantage of his being away from the museum." The sheriff put a hand on Michael's shoulder. "He's very grateful to you all."

The Makers all smiled.

"Still . . . you know you shouldn't be getting involved in police matters," the sheriff said loudly. Everyone in the room could hear her. Then in a whisper she said, "But thanks anyway."

Liv gave Michael and Leo a face that said, "I told you so."

Michael wondered, could she be right that the sheriff wanted them to help solve crimes?

"So, as a reward . . . ," the sheriff started.

"Reward?" Leo echoed with a grin.

"The museum is going to have an art show for Liv's paintings!" the sheriff told them.

Liv jumped up and down. "HOORAY!"

"That's not a real reward," Leo whispered to Michael. "I wanted a cake."

On the way home, Liv talked about all the different paintings she'd make. "Bats at midnight. Black bears in a cave. Blue birds in the sky. Canaries in a field of daffodils . . ."

She was still coming up with ideas when they stopped to go their separate ways.

"See you later," Leo said, heading toward his own apartment.

"Rest up for our next adventure!" Liv called.

Michael smiled. "I can't wait!"

YOU CAN BE A
MYSTERIOUS MAKER
TOO:

KRAFTY KITE

Things to find:

- Two long sticks, called dowels: The dowel for the spine (the up and down one) should be about ⅛ inch thick and 35 inches long. The dowel for the spar (the one across the kite) should be ½ inch thick and a little shorter, about 30 inches long.
- String or twine
- Scissors
- Kitchen-sized garbage bag
- Glue
- Ribbon

Directions:

1. Tie the sticks together in a cross shape. The shorter stick should be one third of the way down from the top of the longer stick. Make sure both sides of the cross stick are equal length. Tie them tightly in this shape by wrapping the twine several times and knotting it tightly. You can use a dab of glue where the sticks meet to make the connection stronger.

2. Cut the garbage bag in a diamond shape to fit the frame. Lay it under your sticks and cut it to fit.

3. Tie the bag to the sticks by tying short twine pieces in tight knots. You don't need glue here. (Liv used glue since hers was a fabric kite. For this one it'll work fine without any glue.)

4. Now you need a flying string. (This is a loose string that you'll attach to the ball of twine when you fly your kite.) First, attach a piece of string to the cross bar. It's going to be loose, so if your dowel is 30 inches, make the string 35 inches long. It should be tied tight to the dowel, about 2 inches from one edge, and then tied to the same spot on the other side. Make sure that it hangs loose. Next, tie a 12-inch piece of string to the first piece of string, going down to the vertical dowel. Tie the other end to the dowel. This one should be loose as well.

5. Loop the ball of string through the flying string. Tie a knot to hold it in place.

6. Tie a piece of ribbon about six times longer than the kite to the bottom for balance.

7. Find a good wind. Have fun!

GLOSSARY

circuit (SUR-kit)—a complete path for an electrical current

consistency (kuhn-SIS-ton-see)—the degree of thickness, firmness, or stickiness

drone (DROHN)—an aircraft without a pilot that is controlled remotely

flashbulb (FLASH-buhlb)—an electric bulb that can be used only once to produce a brief and very bright flash for taking photographs

GPS (GEE PEE ESS)—a system of satellites and devices that people use to find out where they are or to get directions to a place; GPS is short for Global Positioning System

mineral (MIN-ur-uhl)—a solid substance found in the earth that does not come from an animal or plant

program (PROH-gram)—a series of instructions, written in a computer language, that controls the way a computer works

satellite (SAT-uh-lite)—a spacecraft that is sent into orbit around Earth, the moon, or another heavenly body

strobe (STROHB)—a device that produces very brief, high-intensity flashes of light

TALK WITH YOUR FELLOW MAKERS!

1. One of the Mysterious Makers suggests buying a drone instead of making one. Explain why the others don't want to buy one. What are the benefits of making something rather than buying it?

2. How would the book have been different if the Mysterious Makers had called Sheriff Kawasaki from the beginning instead of investigating the crime themselves?

GRAB YOUR MAKER NOTEBOOK!

1. Review the items the Mysterious Makers used in their inventions. What else could you make from the same supplies? Write about how you would make your invention and what it would be used for.

2. Pick a scene in which you disagreed with how a character handled a situation. Rewrite it in the way you think it should have happened.

THE FUN DOESN'T STOP HERE:

Discover more at www.capstonekids.com

- Videos & Contests
- Games & Puzzles
- Friends & Favorites
- Authors & Illustrators

Find cool websites and more books like this one at www.facthound.com. Just type in the Book ID: 9781496546777 and you're ready to go!

READ MORE MAKERS ADVENTURES!